For the Teacher

This reproducible study guide to use in conjunction with the novel *Lizzie Bright and the Buckminster Boy* consists of lessons for guided reading. Written in chapter-by-chapter format, the guide contains a synopsis, pre-reading activities, vocabulary and comprehension exercises, as well as extension activities to be used as follow-up to the novel.

In a homogeneous classroom, whole class instruction with one title is appropriate. In a heterogeneous classroom, reading groups should be formed: each group works on a different novel at its own reading level. Depending upon the length of time devoted to reading in the classroom, each novel, with its guide and accompanying lessons, may be completed in three to six weeks.

Begin using NOVEL-TIES for reading development by distributing the novel and a folder to each child. Distribute duplicated pages of the study guide for students to place in their folders. After examining the cover and glancing through the book, students can participate in several pre-reading activities. Vocabulary questions should be considered prior to reading a chapter; all other work should be done after the chapter has been read. Comprehension questions can be answered orally or in writing. The classroom teacher should determine the amount of work to be assigned, always keeping in mind that readers must be nurtured and that the ultimate goal is encouraging students' love of reading.

The benefits of using NOVEL-TIES are numerous. Students read good literature in the original, rather than in abridged or edited form. The good reading habits, formed by practice in focusing on interpretive comprehension and literary techniques, will be transferred to the books students read independently. Passive readers become active, avid readers.

Novel-Ties® are printed on recycled paper.

SYNOPSIS

The year is 1911 when Reverend and Mrs. Buckminster and their thirteen-year-old son Turner arrive in the small town of Phippsburg, Maine to take up residence in the parsonage. After a brass band heralds their arrival, they are whisked off to a picnic prepared in their honor. The welcome soon cools for Turner when in quick succession he strikes out in an unfamiliar game of high-pitch baseball, fails to leap off a ledge into the sea, is caught skipping rocks at crotchety Mrs. Cobb's picket fence, breaks the nose of Deacon Hurd's son Willis, and is seen standing in his underwear in Mrs. Cobb's kitchen. Turner, who is caught between his elders' expectations that he should behave as a proper minister's son and the ostracism he feels from the boys in the town, can only dream about leaving home and heading west for the Territories.

Life improves for Turner when he meets Lizzie Bright Griffin, a spunky thirteen-year-old resident of Malaga Island, a poor community populated by African Americans just offshore from Phippsburg. When word of their friendship reaches the town elders led by Mr. Stonecrop, a scheming opportunist, a minor scandal ensues. Turner's woes are compounded when his image-conscious father adopts the town's racist point of view and forbids Turner from setting foot on Malaga Island. Adding insult to injury, Turner now must spend several afternoons each week reading or playing hymns for Mrs. Cobb on the organ in her dark, dusty parlor.

When Turner learns that the town elders plan to evict the residents of Malaga Island for the purpose of developing elegant tourist hotels, replacing Phippsburg's declining shipyard business, he is determined to save the Malaga community. He sees an opportunity when old Mrs. Cobb unexpectedly bequeaths him her home: he resolves to give it to Lizzie and the remaining residents of the island. Mr. Stonecrop, Sheriff Elwell, and Deacon Hurd vow that this will not happen. Claiming to act in the town's best interests, they forcibly remove the residents of Malaga Island to Pownal, the state asylum.

Reverend Buckminster, finally understanding the cruelty that is being perpetrated against the residents of Malaga Island, becomes embroiled in a fist fight with Sheriff Elwell. In the ensuing melee, Buckminster hurtles down the granite cliff and sustains an injury from which he never recovers.

At the funeral, Turner has scathing words for the congregation that had already decided to dismiss his father. He and his mother, however, choose to stay on in Phippsburg, living in the house bequeathed to them by Mrs. Cobb. When the Hurd family becomes penniless after Mr. Stonecrop absconds with the townspeople's investments, Mrs. Buckminster invites the Hurd family to live with her and Turner. As soon as the weather permits, Turner visits Pownal to bring Lizzie back with him. To his great sadness, he learns that Lizzie died shortly after being taken to the asylum. The book ends as Turner, borrowing Willis's boat, rows out on the bay where he encounters the whales and allows himself to grieve for all that he has lost.

BACKGROUND INFORMATION

Malaga Island

Malaga Island is located in Casco Bay, near the mouth of the New Meadows River. The island is about a half-mile long by a quarter-mile wide and sits about one hundred yards from the mainland of Phippsburg, Maine. The island is currently uninhabited, but local fishermen use the island to store their lobster traps.

Malaga Island was once a unique community of black and mixed-race individuals in a state that was 99% white. By 1900 the population on the island reached forty-two individuals, and interracial marriages were common. Except for its racial diversity, Malaga resembled many other poor fishing towns on the coast of Maine.

The main source of income for the Malagaites were subsistence fishing and a limited amount of farming. Many mainlanders believed that their livelihoods suffered as they were in direct competition with the fishermen on Malaga Island. These tensions were fueled by rumors of the Malagaites' questionable morals and idleness. In 1903 a missionary family established an informal school on Malaga in order to "reform" its inhabitants.

Tensions between the mainland and the island rose significantly at the turn of the century when tourism was growing on the Maine coast. Malaga became an embarrassment for the mainland. The towns of Harpswell and Phippsburg disowned the community and the island became a ward of the state. In 1912, Governor Plaisted evicted the community of Malaga from their land and homes. All of the homes on the island were razed. Lacking the means to move elsewhere, many of the residents were sent to the Maine School for the Feeble-Minded in Pineland. The island graveyard was dug up and moved to the same institution. Other Malagaites strapped their houses to rafts and drifted them up and down the river, to little avail, in search of a safe port.

To see photographs of residents of the island and of the schoolhouse, visit *NewEnglandAncestors.org*.

PRE-READING ACTIVITIES

1. Preview the book by reading the title and the author's name and by looking at the illustration on the cover. When and where do you think this book takes place? What do you think this book will be about? Will it tell a realistic or a fantastic story? Have you read any other books by the same author?

2. Locate the states of Maine and Massachusetts on a map of the United States. In what part of the country are they found? Then on a map of the New England states, find the city of Boston, Massachusetts, and the town of Phippsburg in Maine. Using the distance scale, calculate how far Phippsburg is from Boston by road. Then trace the water route between the two locations. Why might people prefer to travel by steamer rather than road in the early part of the twentieth century?

3. **Social Studies Connection:** Locate Malaga Island on a map of coastal Maine. Read the Background Information on page two of this study guide and the Author's Note that appears at the end of *Lizzie Bright and the Buckminster Boy*. Based on what you have learned about Malaga Island, make a prediction about what happens to Lizzie Bright, who lives with her grandfather on the island.

4. *Lizzie Bright and the Buckminster Boy* describes the struggles that the son of a minister faces when his family relocates from a large city to a small rural town. What problems do most young people confront when moving to a new community? What unique challenges might a minister's son encounter?

5. When Turner Buckminster finally makes a new friend, he soon finds that his father, as well as the town, disapproves of this relationship. Have you ever been in a situation in which your parents did not approve of a friendship? Why did they disapprove? How would you feel if your parents forbade you to associate with someone?

6. In an interview, the author, Gary Schmidt, said, "I suppose the big reason [that I write for young readers] is that I am fascinated by that moment in a kid's life when she decides that she will take responsibility for a decision . . . ." Tell about a time in your life when you had to take responsibility for a difficult decision. Describe the decision and tell how it affected your life. Looking back, would you make the same decision if you were confronted by a similar problem today? As you read the book, notice why Darwin's theory was controversial in Phillipsburg, Maine.

7. **Science Connection:** Do some research to learn about Charles Darwin and his theory of evolution. Why did his work create controversy when it was first published? Why does it create controversy today? As you read the book, notice why Darwin's theory was controversial in Phillipsburg, Maine.

8. *Lizzie Bright and the Buckminster Boy* was named both a Newbery Honor and a Printz Honor book. Think of award-winning books you have read. What qualities do these books have in common? As you read this novel, decide why it was selected to receive these prestigious awards.

Pre-Reading Questions and Activities (cont.)

9. **Literary Element: Theme**—A novel's theme is its central idea or message. The consequences of rebellion against society's established rules are an important theme in this novel. In a small group, discuss what conformity means and what the consequences can be when people rebel against social rules. Can you think of any instances when taking a stand against community norms and values is worthwhile regardless of the personal cost to you or those you love?

10. Historical fiction is a genre of literature in which fictional characters play out their roles against a background true to a historical period. As you read *Lizzie Bright and the Buckminster Boy*, try to decide which details are historical and which ones were made up by the author to advance the story.

CHAPTER 1

Vocabulary: Draw a line from each word on the left to its definition on the right. Then use the numbered words to fill in the blanks in the sentences below.

1. parsonage
2. deacons
3. meandered
4. chaos
5. reprieve
6. dory
7. resin
8. unison

a. wood flat-bottomed rowboat with high sides
b. temporary relief from danger or trouble
c. simultaneous action
d. church officers who help a minister
e. wandered without any purpose
f. thick substance obtained from certain pine trees
g. home of a minister or parson
h. complete confusion and disorder

. . . .

1. When Jon's presentation was postponed because of a fire drill, he felt as if he had been given a temporary _____.

2. The fisherman rowed out into the bay in search of cod after loading his _____ with nets and bait.

3. The women of the Ladies Sewing Circle made new curtains to decorate rooms of the _____ before the arrival of the new minister and his family.

4. It was hard to remove the _____ that had dripped on the windshield from the pine tree near our driveway.

5. Complete _____ erupted in the auditorium when someone yelled, "Fire."

6. The chorus practiced long and hard so that they could sing in _____.

7. It was difficult to follow the path through the woods because it _____ around large outcroppings of granite, fallen trees, and broken stumps.

8. After interviewing several candidates, the _____ met to choose the new pastor of the First Congregational Church.

> Read to find out what happens when Reverend Buckminster and his family arrive in Phippsburg.

Chapter 1 (cont.)

Questions:

1. How did Turner's reception in Phippsburg differ from that of his parents?

2. What were Turner's first three failures in Phippsburg? Why did each happen?

3. Why did Mrs. Cobb object so strenuously to Turner's behavior? What did she propose to do about it?

4. How was Turner's day rescued from being a total disaster?

5. How did Lizzie Bright's feelings about living on Malaga Island compare to Turner's feelings about living in Phippsburg?

Questions for Discussion:

1. Do you think the child of a clergyman is judged by a higher moral standard than other children are?

2. Why do you think the populace of Phippsburg gave the new minister and his wife such a rousing welcome?

3. Do you think Turner should have asked Willis for some pointers on how to hit a soft ball? Why wouldn't he ask?

4. Do you think Turner deserved any of the treatment he received from his peers in Phippsburg?

5. What did Mrs. Hurd mean when she asked Turner if the number at the end of his name made him feel as if he were looking through prison bars? Have you ever felt the same way about your own life?

Literary Devices:

I. *Metaphor*—A metaphor is an implied or suggested comparison of two unlike objects. For example, Mrs. Hurd when speaking about Mrs. Cobb and herself says:

> She's more thunder than lightning. I'm more . . . a cloud. A wispy one.

What is being compared?

_____

_____

What does this reveal about each of the women?

_____

_____

_____

Chapter 1 (cont.)

II. *Personification*—Personification is a figure of speech in which an author grants human qualities to a nonhuman object. For example:

> She [Lizzie Bright] let her weight into it [a young pine tree], back and forth, and the whole heap of Malaga Island rushed beneath her—ocean, sand, rock, scrub, mudflat, pale little crab, all rushing back and forth as the soft boughs laid their gentle, dry hands against her laughing face.

What is being personified?

_____

How does Lizzie's encounter with the pine echo Turner's encounter with Mrs. Hurd?

_____

_____

III. *Symbolism*—A symbol in literature is an object, event, or person that represents an idea or set of ideas. What does Mrs. Hurd's house symbolize?

_____

_____

IV. *Foreshadowing*—Foreshadowing is the use of clues by the author to prepare the reader for future developments of the plot. What might be foreshadowed when the man lays his hand on the pistol hidden beneath his frock coat?

_____

_____

Writing Activities:

1. Pretend you are Tucker. Write a letter to your best friend in Boston describing your first two days in Phippsburg.

2. Reread the opening paragraph of this chapter and notice how Turner describes Phippsburg, Maine using each of his five senses. Choose a place that you know well. Write a one-paragraph description in which you capture its essence using the senses of touch, taste, smell, hearing, and sight.

CHAPTER 2

Vocabulary: Antonyms are words with opposite meanings. Draw a line from each word in column A to its antonym in column B. Then use the words in column A to fill in the blanks in the sentences below.

A		B	
1.	shanties	a.	millionaires
2.	paupers	b.	solemn
3.	daft	c.	destruction
4.	uproarious	d.	native
5.	salvation	e.	dispensing
6.	tourist	f.	mansions
7.	ebb	g.	strengthen
8.	hoarding	h.	sane

. . . .

1. Noticing the camera on his shoulder and the guide book in his hand, we assumed he was a(n) _____.

2. The crowd burst out in _____ laughter when the clown tripped over his large shoes.

3. The minister promised _____ to his flock if they prayed and led good lives.

4. My brother's unusual behavior on the football field seemed _____ to most observers until he scored a touchdown.

5. Afraid that a hurricane would knock out all the electrical lines, people began _____ candles and flashlights.

6. The soldiers' courage began to _____ when they found themselves totally surrounded by enemy forces.

7. When the banks failed during the Great Depression, many formerly wealthy people became _____.

8. The town council voted to bulldoze the row of ramshackle _____ and replace them with sturdy, elegant homes for the rich.

> Read to learn about Mr. Stonecrop's plan for Malaga Island.

Chapter 2 (cont.)

Questions:

1. Why did Mr. Stonecrop argue for the destruction of all the homes on Malaga Island?

2. Why was Turner given the task of reading to Mrs. Cobb daily?

3. Why did Turner fight Willis? How did Turner feel after the fight?

4. Why did Lizzie begin to cry when watching the crab?

5. Why did the town elders of Phippsburg visit Malaga Island? How did they justify their decision to Reverend Griffin?

6. Why did Reverend Griffin take the Phippsburg elders to the graveyard? How did the men in frock coats respond?

Questions for Discussion:

1. Why do you think Sheriff Elwell spoke openly to the men in frock coats about his prejudice against the people of Malaga Island?

2. In your opinion why did Willis and his friends tease Turner?

3. Why do you think the community of Phippsburg could act against the wishes of people who lived on Malaga Island?

4. Why do you think Reverend Griffin agreed to carry out the wishes of the men in frock coats? Why didn't Reverend Buckminster speak up in defense of the people who lived on Malaga Island?

5. What do you think Lizzie meant when she told herself that "she would not ebb"? How might this decision affect her actions?

Literary Devices:

I. *Symbol*—What do each of the following symbolize?

   • a starched white shirt _____

   _____

   • the frock coats_____

   _____

   • the crab Zerubabel_____

   _____

   • the gulls _____

   _____

Chapter 2 (cont.)

II. *Allusion*—An allusion in literature is a reference to a familiar person, place, or event. Why do you think the author includes so many allusions to religion and biblical characters?

_____

_____

Find an example of an allusion in this chapter and explain its meaning.

_____

_____

III. *Personification*—Throughout *Lizzie Bright and the Buckminster Boy*, the author treats the sea breeze as if it were a character. Copy the following chart on another sheet of paper. Use it to keep a record of how the author brings the sea breeze to life. For each example, describe the role and purpose of the sea breeze at that moment in the novel.

Page	What the Sea Breeze Does	Role and Purpose of the Sea Breeze

IV. *Irony*—Irony refers to a twist of fate or an event that is the opposite of that which is expected. What is ironic about the plans that the church-going members of the Phippsburg community have for Malaga Island?

_____

_____

_____

Writing Activity:

After the fight with Willis, Turner experiences both pain and satisfaction. Write about a time when you experienced two conflicting emotions. Describe how and why you felt both ways.

Chapter 2 (cont.)

Literary Element: Characterization

Fill in the chart below with information about the major characters you have met in the first two chapters. Add to the chart as you learn about other important characters in the book.

Character	Information
Turner	
Reverend Buckminster	
Deacon Hurd	
Willis	
Lizzie Bright	
Mrs. Cobb	
Mrs. Hurd	
Mr. Stonecrop	
Reverend Griffin	

CHAPTERS 3, 4

Vocabulary: Synonyms are words with similar meanings. Draw a line from each word in column A to its synonym in column B. Then use the words in column A to fill in the blanks in the sentences below.

A		B	
1.	brawl	a.	dark
2.	scent	b.	scramble
3.	murky	c.	fragrance
4.	stunned	d.	guilt
5.	clamber	e.	wrestling
6.	grappling	f.	fight
7.	brink	g.	edge
8.	remorse	h.	surprised

· ·

1. Despite all the complaints, the builder felt no _____ for chopping down all the trees to make room for the apartment complex.

2. After _____ with the math problem for over an hour, I went to my older sister for help.

3. When the auto assembly plant closed, causing many workers to lose their jobs, the entire town stood on the _____ of collapse.

4. It was impossible to see the fish because the water at the bottom of the pond was so _____.

5. The teacher stepped in between the boys, who were teasing one another, before a noisy _____ broke out.

6. The _____ of the pine trees reminded me of the childhood summers I spent with my family in a cabin in the woods.

7. I was _____ when I read in the newspaper that our seemingly honest neighbor had been arrested for bank robbery.

8. The path to the beach was so steep and rocky that we had to _____ down carefully for fear of falling.

> Read to find out about Turner's first visit to Malaga Island.

Chapters 3, 4 (cont.)

Questions:

1. Why did Reverend Buckminster heap more punishments upon his son?

2. Why did Turner climb down the cliffs and go to the seashore?

3. Why did Lizzie pitch stones to Turner?

4. What evidence showed that Turner's mother realized how hard it was for her son to be the minister's son?

5. Why was Turner amazed by Mrs. Hurd's advice?

6. How did Turner feel when he and Lizzie reached Malaga Island? How did his reception there differ from the one he received in Phippsburg?

7. How did Mr. Stonecrop persuade Reverend Buckminster to adopt the "interest of the town" when it came to Malaga Island? Why did Turner feel as if Mr. Stonecrop was using him as a prop in a play?

Questions for Discussion:

1. Do you think Reverend Buckminster made any attempt to understand his son? Should Turner do more to please his father?

2. Do you think Reverend Buckminster truly believed in all he preached or was he just playing the role that was expected of him, as Turner suspected?

3. In your opinion, what did Reverend Griffin think of Turner's memorized passage from the Bible? What do you think this passage revealed about Turner?

4. Why do you think the town elders and Reverend Buckminster were so shocked by Turner's visit to Malaga Island?

5. What do you think will happen now that Reverend Buckminster has agreed to support Mr. Stonecrop's plans for Malaga Island?

Literary Devices:

I. *Simile*—A simile is a figure of speech in which two unlike objects are compared using the words "like" or "as." For example:

> He was as polite as an angel all the way through the roast and potatoes . . . .
> While carrying out the dishes, he was as helpful as St. Timothy.

What is being compared?

_____

Why are these meaningful comparisons?

_____

_____

Chapters 3, 4 (cont.)

II. *Sarcasm*—Sarcasm is praise that actually means the opposite of what is said, and is meant as ridicule. For example, Reverend Buckminster comments:

> You were in your underwear in Mrs. Cobb's kitchen. Let us praise God that decency reigns.

What is sarcastic about Reverend Buckminster's observation?

_____

_____

What does he really mean by his remark?

_____

_____

III. *Personification*—What is being personified in this passage:

> They [the raindrops] played across the coast all through the night,
> until the soft new day shrugged itself awake, tried on amethyst
> and lavender for a while, and finally decided on pale yellow.

What image does this create in your mind?

_____

_____

Literary Element: Characterization

Compare Lizzie and Turner in a Venn diagram, such as the one below. Record the ways these two characters are alike in the overlapping part of the circles. Record their differences in the outer portion of each circle.

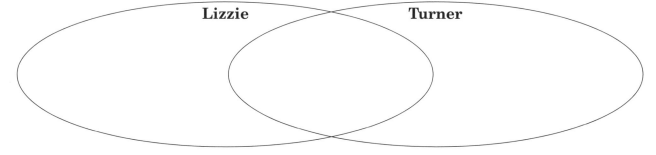

Writing Activity:

Tell about a friendship that has brightened your life. Describe where, when, and how you met your friend. Then write about some of the activities you enjoy doing together.

CHAPTER 5

Vocabulary: Analogies are equations in which the first pair of words has the same relationship as the second pair of words. For example: BLUEBERRY is to FRUIT as SPINACH is to VEGETABLE. In each pair, the first word names an example of the second word. Choose the best word to complete each of the following analogies.

1. PRESIDENT is to CONSTITUENCY as _____ is to CONGREGATION.

   a. educator   b. minister   c. senator   d. voter

2. FRONT is to BOW as REAR is to _____.

   a. dory   b. deck   c. sloop   d. stern

3. SEA is to VAST as WHALE is to _____.

   a. gargantuan   b. flippers   c. clumsy   d. maelstrom

4. _____ is to OCEAN as POND is to LAKE.

   a. glacier   b. puddle   c. bay   d. river

5. HOURS is to DAY as YEARS is to _____.

   a. minute   b. century   c. moment   d. month

6. _____ is to BOTTOM as LIGHT is to DARKNESS.

   a. surface   b. treasure   c. median   d. infinity

7. OMEN is to SIGN as _____ is to PRAYER.

   a. fortune   b. amen   c. benediction   d. curse

8. GRACEFUL is to _____ as POLITE is to RUDE.

   a. subtle   b. crude   c. gentle   d. awkward

Read to find out what happens when Lizzie and Turner climb the granite ledges.

Questions:

1. How did Turner manage to get around his father's latest rule?

2. Why did Turner find it difficult to reach Malaga in the dory?

Chapter 5 (cont.)

3. While rowing to Malaga Island, how did a moment of panic for Turner turn into one of peace and joy?

4. How did the townspeople greet Lizzie and Turner's return? What were his parents' reactions?

5. Why did Reverend Buckminster accuse Turner of being impertinent?

6. How did Reverend Buckminster respond to Mr. Stonecrop's threat?

Questions for Discussion:

1. Was Turner wrong in obeying the letter but not the spirit of his father's commandment?

2. Why do you think Turner's encounter with the whales seemed to take on the importance of a religious experience?

3. Why did Turner feel that his father was "much smaller than he had been before"?

4. Do you think Reverend Buckminster will honor Mr. Stonecrop's threat?

Literary Element: Mood

Mood is the feeling that a piece of literature creates in a reader. Reread the section of the chapter that describes the arrival of Turner and Lizzie at the dock. What mood is the author trying to create? What words and phrases help create this mood?

_____

_____

_____

Literary Devices:

I. *Metaphor*—What is being compared in the following metaphor?

> In the moonlight he [Turner] saw a silver spray burst up into the air, a shower of diamond dust . . . . Turner knew, or felt the vastness of the whales.

_____

Why is this an apt comparison?

_____

Chapter 5 (cont.)

II. *Personification*—What is being personified in the following passage:

> The moon had roused herself fully out of the sea and was tossing her silver bedclothes all around.

_____

Why is this better than saying, "The moon rose, casting its glow all around"?

_____

_____

III. *Refrain*—A refrain is a repeated phrase or verse that is found more often in music than in prose. Why do you think Turner kept repeating variations of the following phrase:

> He had looked into the eyes of a whale.

_____

_____

Why was Turner's encounter with the whale significant?

_____

_____

Writing Activity:

Imagine you are Turner and write a journal entry describing your thoughts and feelings at the end of the day when you and Lizzie were rescued on the bay.

CHAPTERS 6, 7

Vocabulary: Use the words in the Word Box and the clues below to complete the crossword puzzle.

> *WORD BOX*
>
> | | | | |
> |---|---|---|---|
> | amaze | dull | grace | hymn |
> | dawdled | dwindle | haughty | malice |
> | dirge | exiled | hero | melancholy |
> | disdain | eyed | humiliation | melee |

Across

1. proud
3. person admired for brave and noble deeds
4. sad; gloomy
5. evil intent
6. grow smaller in size
9. astonish; surprise
10. acted slowly
11. banished from a native land
12. slow, mournful tune

Down

1. embarrassment
2. beauty of motion
3. song in praise of God
5. confused fight involving many people
6. scorn or haughty contempt
7. boring; monotonous
8. noticed; looked at carefully

> Read to find out how Reverend Buckminster responds to Mr. Stonecrop's plan for Malaga Island.

Chapters 6, 7 (cont.)

Questions:

1. Why did Reverend Buckminster choose the fall of Jericho as the topic for Sunday's sermon?
2. Why did Turner find Sundays dreary? What helped to brighten his mood?
3. Why did Turner carefully choose the hymns he played for Mrs. Cobb?
4. Why did Reverend Buckminster slap his son? How did Turner try to justify his "disobedience"?
5. Why did Lizzie risk a visit to Turner's house?
6. Why did Turner begin to look forward to his visits to Mrs. Cobb?
7. Why did Turner's organ playing suffer on the day he saw Mrs. Hurd's shutters painted green?
8. According to Turner's mother, why was Mrs. Hurd committed to an insane asylum?
9. Why didn't Turner attend the Phippsburg school? How did he feel about his assignments?
10. What surprising discovery did Turner make when he ran down to the New Meadows?

Questions for Discussion:

1. Do you think Turner deserved his father's harsh punishment?
2. Why do you think Sheriff Elwell lied to Lizzie and her grandfather?
3. Why do you think Mrs. Cobb tolerated Lizzie's visits? Why didn't she speak directly to Lizzie?
4. Why do you think Mrs. Buckminster told Turner the facts behind Mrs. Hurd's disappearance?
5. Why do you think Lizzie didn't respond to Turner's wave of greeting from across the New Meadows?

Literary Devices:

I. *Simile*—What is being compared in the following simile?

> The grim silence circled the room like an eager tiger. It flicked its tail greedily at them, circling, circling, circling.

_____

Why is this better than saying, "Reverend Buckminster's silence revealed his growing anger toward Turner."

_____
_____
_____

Chapters 6, 7 (cont.)

II. *Allusion*—The tale of Aeneas is a famous epic poem written long ago by the famous poet Virgil. Latin students in high school and college still read and translate the adventures of Aeneas today. To read a summary of the *Aeneid*, visit this high school website: http://chaipo.tripod.com/. After you have read the summary, write a paragraph in which you explain why Turner could identify with Aeneas.

Music Connection:

You can pretend you are sitting in Mrs. Cobb's dusty parlor and listen to the hymn "Shall We Gather at the River" by visiting this website: http://www.*cyberhymnal.org*. After reading the text of the lyrics and listening to all four verses, write a paragraph explaining why you think Reverend Griffin would lead the residents of Malaga in singing this song as they watched the Tripp family float away from the Island.

Writing Activities:

1. Write about a time in your life when major changes or losses occurred. Describe the changes and tell how they made you feel. Then tell about a person or an event that helped you move forward with life.

2. Turner's assignment after translating and summarizing 100 lines of the *Aeneid* is to rewrite the summary from the perspective of four major characters in the story. Do the same with an episode from Chapter Seven or Eight. Begin by writing a straightforward summary telling what happened. The rewrite the summary two or three times from the perspective of several different characters.

CHAPTERS 8, 9

Vocabulary: Read each group of words. Choose the one word that does not belong with the others and cross it out. On the lines below the words, tell how the rest of the words are alike.

1. maples   aspens   beeches   leaves

   These words are alike because they all _____

2. conflagration   smolder   kindling   blaze

   These words are alike because they all _____

3. Charles Darwin   Jim Hawkins   Sinbad   Huck Finn

   These words are alike because they all _____

4. shutters   curtains   blinds   porch

   These words are alike because they all _____

5. cemetery   eulogy   pallbearers   theater

   These words are alike because they all _____

6. gust   jig   do-si-do   promenade

   These words are alike because they all _____

7. sprinted   raced   accelerated   hovered

   These words are alike because they all _____

> Read to find out about Mrs. Cobb's last words and last wishes.

Questions:

1. Why did Mr. Stonecrop insist that Reverend Buckminster write a letter to Governor Plaistead?

2. Why did Reverend Buckminster hesitate before giving Turner *The Origin of Species*? What promise did Turner have to make before he was allowed to read it?

Chapters 8, 9 (cont.)

3. How did Turner surprise the people of Phippsburg at the last game of the season?

4. What final regret did Mrs. Cobb express to Lizzie and Turner? Why did Lizzie and Turner debate over Mrs. Cobb's actual last words?

5. Why were Mr. Stonecrop and the townspeople of Phippsburg stunned by Mrs. Cobb's will?

6. Why did Turner convince Mr. Eason to row him to Malaga? Why was Lizzie staying with the Easons?

Questions for Discussion:

1. What do you think Reverend Buckminster meant when he said that "Books can ignite fires in your mind, because they carry ideas for kindling, and art for matches"?

2. Why do you think Mrs. Cobb told Turner that he didn't have to be a minister's son all the time? What did this reveal about her?

3. Why do you think Turner let Willis Hurd strike him out?

4. Why do you think Willis was painting his grandmother's shutters? Will he and Turner ever become friends?

5. Why do you think Reverend Buckminster changed Mrs. Cobb's last words when he was delivering his sermon?

6. What do you think Turner plans to do with Mrs. Cobb's house?

Literary Devices:

I. *Simile*—What two comparisons are being made in the following passage?

> Still the disapproval of the First Congregational stifled him like the silence a fog brings upon the ocean. And when his father spoke again, he sounded like an invisible buoy. "We will do what is good and honorable in the Lord's eyes."

_____

_____

What critical change does the author signal in this comparison?

_____

_____

Chapters 8, 9 (cont.)

II. *Symbolism*—What did the granite ledges near the shore in Phippsburg symbolize?

_____

Why do you think the originator of the plan for Malaga Island was called "Mr. Stonecrop"?

_____

_____

_____

Writing Activity:

An obituary is a brief summary of someone's life that often appears in a newspaper after the person's death. Become familiar with the form by reading several obituaries in a local newspaper. Then write an obituary for Mrs. Cobb. Include information on her interests, her family, and her life. In addition to including information found in *Lizzie Bright and the Buckminster Boy*, you may also make up some details about her history.

CHAPTER 10

Vocabulary: Use the context to help you figure out the meaning of the underlined word in each of the following sentences. Then compare your definitions with those you find in a dictionary.

1. So that I would not insult my friend, I <u>discreetly</u> moved the furniture in my room back to the place it had been.

    Your definition_____

    Dictionary definition _____

2. The detectives roped off the scene of the <u>homicide</u> so they could collect any information they could about the person who had been killed.

    Your definition_____

    Dictionary definition _____

3. The coach warned his team that a <u>lackadaisical</u> attitude could cause his team to lose all of their games.

    Your definition_____

    Dictionary definition _____

4. Jack <u>groped</u> for the light switch in the long, dark hallway.

    Your definition_____

    Dictionary definition _____

5. My brother's <u>grimace</u> revealed that he had seriously sprained his ankle.

    Your definition_____

    Dictionary definition _____

6. The boxer raised his gloves, trying to <u>ward</u> off the shower of blows thrown by the other fighter.

    Your definition_____

    Dictionary definition _____

> Read to find out what happens when Turner reveals his plan for Mrs. Cobb's house.

Chapter 10 (cont.)

Questions:

1. Why did Lizzie tell Turner that he never looked at things straight?
2. How did Mr. Stonecrop and Reverend Buckminster each react when Turner announced his plan for Mrs. Cobb's house?
3. What evidence showed that many of First Congregational's parishioners did not approve of Turner's plan for Mrs. Cobb's house?
4. How did Turner interpret Willis's whispered warning following the service?
5. How did Turner become trapped in Mrs. Cobb's house? How did he escape?
6. Why did Sheriff Elwell fire a shotgun at Turner? How did this cause Reverend Buckminster's terrible accident?
7. Why did Turner fight Sheriff Elwell?

Questions for Discussion:

1. Why do you think Reverend Buckminster decided to risk supporting his son against Mr. Stonecrop and his plans for Mrs. Cobb's house?
2. Do you think Willis had anything to do with trapping Turner in the cupola?
3. Do you think it is more important to live by a set of ethics or to live in the "here and now" as Mr. Stonecrop suggested?

Literary Device: Cliffhanger

A cliffhanger is a device borrowed from silent serialized films in which an episode ended at a moment of great suspense. In a book it usually appears at the end of a chapter to encourage the reader to continue on in the book. What is the cliffhanger at the end of Chapter Ten?

_____

_____

Literary Element: Climax

The climax of a novel is the moment of greatest interest or excitement. It is at the point where interest in the outcome is the highest. What do you think is the climax of *Lizzie Bright and the Buckminster Boy*?

_____

_____

Chapter 10 (cont.)

Writing Activities:

1. Write a news story about the forced removal of the residents of Malaga Island. Use as a model the Portland newspaper article that is found at the beginning of Chapter Eight. In your article, be sure to include details that cover the 5 W's of good reporting—Who?, What?, Where?, Why?, and When? Don't forget to add a headline and a byline.

2. When a person dies, friends of the family often send a condolence card and write a note. Pretend that you are Tucker's friend. Create a card and add a note in which you express your sympathy for the death of his father.

CHAPTERS 11, 12

Vocabulary: Choose a word from the Word Box to replace each underlined word or phrase with a more descriptive word that has a similar meaning. Write the word you choose on the line below the sentence.

WORD BOX		
absconding	dispatched	talisman
ample	feeble	thwarted

1. Letting hunger come before reason, the burglar made himself a sandwich before <u>disappearing suddenly</u> with the cash.

   _____

2. Clearly my brother had gained some weight as his belt could barely reach around his <u>large</u> waistline.

   _____

3. Liz carefully wrapped the four-leaf clover in a napkin and tucked it in her pocket hoping that this <u>magic charm</u> would bring her good luck on the test.

   _____

4. The elderly man became so <u>weak</u> after a long illness that he needed nursing care.

   _____

5. Our plan to go camping was <u>blocked</u> for several days because of rain and high winds.

   _____

6. On Friday afternoons, Mr. Hill <u>quickly finished</u> all the work on his desk so that he could start his weekend early.

   _____

   Read to find out what happens to Lizzie at Pownal Home for the Feeble-Minded.

Chapters 11, 12 (cont.)

Questions:

1. Why did Deacon Hurd convene a deacons' meeting?

2. Why did Mr. Newton express his regrets at the deacons' meeting?

3. Why were the remains of the Malaga Island residents reburied at Pownal?

4. Why was the minister from Bath sorry that he had invited Turner to address the congregation at Reverend Buckminster's funeral?

5. What evidence showed that some of the congregation agreed with Turner?

6. Why did the matron at Pownal inform Turner and Mr. Newton that it was impossible to see Lizzie?

7. Why did Mr. Stonecrop suddenly leave Phippsburg? Why did his departure have a bad effect on many of the people in town?

8. Why did Turner take the tender out in the bay alone? Why did he weep?

Questions for Discussion:

1. Do you agree with Deacon Hurd or Mr. Newton about the nature of a minister's role?

2. Why might it be supposed that Willis had a change of heart?

3. Do you think that those in the congregation who supported Turner might have done more on his behalf?

4. What do you think Mr. Newton meant when he told Turner that he would always be a minister's son?

5. In your opinion, what was it that Turner saw in both the eyes of his father and the eyes of the whale?

6. What do you think it means to "look at something straight on?" Why is it often so difficult to do this?

Literary Devices:

I. *Symbolism*—What did the smoke and ashes from Malaga Island symbolize?

_____

_____

_____

Chapters 11, 12 (cont.)

II. *Foreshadowing*—Reread Turner's imaginary conversation with Lizzie right after the deacons' meeting. How do her comments foreshadow her fate at Pownal?

_____

_____

III. *Proverb*—A proverb is an old and often repeated short saying that contains wise advice. For example:

The apple doesn't fall far [from the tree].

What was a member of the congregation really saying about Turner at the conclusion of his father's funeral?

_____

_____

Was this remark meant to be complimentary or disparaging?

_____

Literary Element: Theme

A *theme* is a central message in a novel. One theme of *Lizzie Bright and the Buckminster Boy* is the importance of discovering one's true identity or self. Another theme is the importance of friendship and connecting with other people and living things in the natural world. Using Turner, Reverend Buckminster, Lizzie, Mrs. Hurd, Mrs. Cobb, and Willis, tell how the events in this novel illustrate both themes.

Writing Activities:

1. Imagine that you are Turner. Write a journal entry in which you express your feelings about the death of your father and Lizzie.

2. Throughout the last half of the novel, Turner and Mrs. Buckminster seem to grow closer as she lends Turner her support in his efforts to discover his own identity as someone other than the minster's son. Describe someone who has helped you to learn more about yourself. Explain how this person encouraged you to take responsibility for the person you are and want to be.

CLOZE ACTIVITY

The following passage is taken from Chapter Twelve of the book. Read the entire passage before filling in the blanks. Then reread the passage and fill in each blank with a word that makes sense. Finally, you may compare your language with that of the author.

The whales waited for him. Sometimes they went below the surface and came up _____,[1] but mostly they waited for him in _____[2] puny tender. The gulls circled them like _____[3] halos, until Turner shipped his oars and _____[4] the swells carry him.

He could not _____[5] if the waves were drifting him closer _____[6] the whales or if the whales were _____[7] closer to him. In any case, soon _____[8] was so close that when he held _____[9] his hand over the water, all he _____[10] to do was reach down and he _____[11] touch the dark gray rubber of a _____[12] skin, stretched to perfect tautness, smelling _____[13] the deep sea. He felt more than _____[14] the size of the whales, and the _____[15] knowing within them.

He turned from one _____[16] another, their sea-washed eyes open and watching, _____[17] then finally he leaned out. And he _____[18] the cool, wet, perfect smoothness of whale.

_____[19] he knew. Then he knew.

The knowledge _____[20] his father's eyes and in the whales' _____.[21]

The world turns and the world spins, _____[22] tide runs in and the tide runs _____,[23] and there is nothing in the world _____[24] beautiful and more wonderful in all its _____[25] forms than two souls who look at _____[26] other straight on. And there is nothing _____[27] woeful and soul-saddening than when they are _____.[28] Turner knew that everything in the world _____[29] in the touch, and everything in the _____[30] laments in the losing.

And he had lost Malaga.

POST-READING ACTIVITIES AND DISCUSSION QUESTIONS

1. Return to the chart on the personification of the sea breeze that you began on page ten of this study guide. Add any more examples that you found as you continued to read the book. Compare your examples with those of your classmates. Then discuss the possible reasons why the author chose to give the sea breeze human characteristics.

2. Return to the characterization chart that you began on page eleven of this study guide. Fill in additional information about the characters and compare your chart with those of your classmates.

3. Return to the title page and reread the title of the book. Why do you think the author used only Lizzie's first and middle names and referred to Turner as the Buckminster Boy in the title? What might be another appropriate title for this novel?

4. Sometimes authors choose to identify their characters with names that carry a special connotation or meaning. What comes to your mind when you think about the names of each of the following characters: *Turner, Bright, Stonecrop, Buckminster, Newton Tripp*. Then using what you know about the character and his or her personality and actions, tell why you think the name is or is not appropriate.

5. Decide on a creative way that you would like to share *Lizzie Bright and the Buckminster Boy* with others. You might write up an interview with one of the characters. You could also create an advertisement to "sell" the book to your classmates, dramatize a chapter, design a book cover, or make a diorama showing your favorite scene from the book. Choose one of these ideas or come up with your own. Then present your finished project to others who might enjoy reading this book.

6. **Fluency Practice:** Choose a favorite chapter in the book. Work with a partner or a small group to practice a dramatic reading of the chapter. One option is to alternate reading several pages. Another is to do a Readers Theater. If you select the latter option, choose a chapter that has a lot of dialogue. As you practice, pay attention to phrasing and expression; you may also wish to make a tape recording to help you assess your oral reading. When you are ready, share your dramatic reading with the class.

7. **Pair/Share:** The houses in *Lizzie Bright and the Buckminster Boy* are significant, almost conveying a character of their own as they also reflect the character of their inhabitants. Work with a partner to record all you can about the houses of each of the following characters: Lizzie, Turner, Mrs. Hurd, Mrs. Cobb, Mr. Tripp. Compare your notes with those of others in your classroom.

Post-Reading Activities and Discussion Questions (cont.)

8. *Lizzie Bright and the Buckminster Boy* is a fictional story based on a true event that happened on Malaga Island in 1912. Gary Schmidt, the author, felt that this little known story needed to be told not only to preserve and expose this moment in history, but also so that readers could learn from it. Do you think attitudes have changed since the last century? What do you think remains to be done to address issues of racism, prejudice, and discrimination?

9. Were you satisfied with the ending of the book? If so, tell why you liked it. If not, tell how you would have preferred the book to end.

10. Have a classroom debate to argue over the positive and negative aspects of the following proposition:

    Every individual is obligated to act upon moral issues, despite the consequences.

11. **Literature Circle:** Have a literature circle discussion in which you tell your personal reactions to *Lizzie Bright and the Buckminster Boy*. Here are some questions and sentence starters to help your literature circle begin a discussion.

    • How are you like Turner or Lizzie? How are you different?
    • Do you find the characters in the novel realistic? Why or why not?
    • Which character did you like the most? The least?
    • Who else would you like to read this novel? Why?
    • What aspects of the book would you like to discuss with the author?
    • How did this work of historical fiction relate to issues in the world today?
    • I would have liked to see . . .
    • I wonder . . .
    • Turner learned that . . .
    • I learned that . . .

SUGGESTIONS FOR FURTHER READING

Alvarez, Julia. *Before We Were Free*. Random House.

Armistead, John. *The $66 Summer*. Milkweed Editions.

_____. *The Return of Gabriel*. Milkweed Editions.

* Choldenko, Gennifer. *Al Capone Does My Shirts*. Penguin.

* Curtis, Christopher Paul. *Bud, Not Buddy*. Random House.

* _____. *The Watsons Go to Birmingham–1963*. Random House.

* De Angeli, Marguerite. *The Door in the Wall*. Random House.

Elliot, Laura Malone. *Flying South*. HarperCollins.

English, Karen. *Francie*. Farrar, Straus & Giroux

Going, K.L. *The Liberation of Gabriel King*. Putnam.

* Green, Bette. *Philip Hall Likes Me, I Reckon Maybe*. Random House.

_____. *Get Out of Here, Philip Hall*. Random House.

* Henkes, Kevin. *Olive's Ocean*. HarperCollins.

Mead, Alice. *Year of No Rain*. Random House.

* Miklowitz, Gloria. *The War Between the Classes*. Random House.

* Newfeld, John. *Edgar Allen*. Penguin.

Park, Linda Sue. *When My Name Was Keoko*. Random House.

Peck, Richard. *The River Between Us*. Putnam.

Rodman, Mary Ann. *Yankee Girl*. Farrar, Straus & Giroux.

Staples, Suzanne Fisher. *Dangerous Skies*. HarperCollins.

* Taylor, Mildred D. *The Friendship*. Penguin.

* _____. *Mississippi Bridge*. Penguin.

_____. *The Road to Memphis*. Penguin.

* _____. *Roll of Thunder, Hear My Cry*. Penguin.

Other Books by Gary D. Schmidt

Anson's Way. Houghton Mifflin.

First Boy. Random House.

Pilgrim's Progress: A Retelling. Wm. B. Eerdmans.

Saint Ciaran. Wm. B. Eerdmans.

The Sin Eater. Penguin.

Straw into Gold. Houghton Mifflin.

William Bradford, Plymouth's Faithful Pilgrim. Wm. B. Eerdmans.

* NOVEL-TIES study guides are available for these titles.

ANSWER KEY

Chapter 1

Vocabulary: 1. g 2. d 3. e 4. h 5. b 6. a 7. f 8. c; 1. reprieve 2. dory 3. parsonage 4. resin 5. chaos 6. unison 7. meandered 8. deacons

Questions: 1. Turner was greeted with hesitation and skepticism by the children in Phippsburg while his parents were warmly welcomed and treated with great respect. 2. Turner's first failure was to strike out during the welcome picnic. This happened because he was used to playing hardball instead of slow pitch baseball. His second failure was his inability to jump off a steep granite cliff into the ocean because of fear. His third failure was to be caught skipping a stone that accidentally hit Mrs. Cobb's picket fence while walking down the main street of Phippsburg without his shirt on. 3. Mrs. Cobb objected to Turner's behavior because he was the minister's son; she felt he should set a good example for others in the town. She said she was going to complain to his father about his behavior. 4. Just when Turner thought his day had reached rock bottom, Mrs. Hurd, the mother of Deacon Hurd, expressed her understanding of the boy's plight and offered him solace. 5. Lizzie loved everything about living on Malaga, and felt she belonged there. Turner strongly disliked living in Phippsburg, and as an outsider, felt he would never belong.

Chapter 2

Vocabulary: 1. f 2. a 3. h 4. b 5. c 6. d 7. g 8. e; 1. tourist 2. uproarious 3. salvation 4. daft 5. hoarding 6. ebb 7. paupers 7. shanties

Questions: 1. Mr. Stonecrop, the richest resident of Phippsburg and owner of the shipyard, felt the days of shipbuilding were coming to an end and that Phippsburg needed to develop a new industry, such as tourism. He felt a resort site could never be developed until the hovels and residents of Malaga Island were removed. 3. Turner punched Willis because he was tired of being taunted. Even though he was beaten, Turner felt some satisfaction that he had stood up for himself and hit Willis. 4. Lizzie began to cry because it didn't seem fair that the crab, which was such a marvelous creature in nature, was so violently and unexpectedly destroyed. 5. The town elders of Phippsburg visited Malaga Island to inform Reverend Griffin of their plan to take down all the shanties on the island and move its inhabitants. They justified this by telling Reverend Griffin that when times change, people must change, too. They said the law was on their side because no one had a registered deed to land on the island. 6. Reverend Griffin took the elders to the graveyard as proof that the ancestors of the inhabitants had lived on the island for generations, which give them a moral if not legal right to live there. He believed that this served the purpose of an actual deed. The elders were not impressed and saw the cemetery as one more thing that would have to be cleared away.

Chapters 3, 4

Vocabulary: 1. f 2. c 3. a 4. h 5. b 6. e 7. g 8. d; 1. remorse 2. grappling 3. brink 4. murky 5. brawl 6. scent 7. stunned 8. clamber

Questions: 1. Reverend Buckminster heaped more punishment upon his son because he disapproved of his brawling with Willis and was appalled that Mrs. Cobb saw him standing in his underwear in her kitchen. 2. Turner climbed down the granite cliffs to the shore in order to find an escape from the pressure of living up to the standard of being the minister's son in Phippsburg. 3. Lizzie pitched stones to Turner to help him learn how to hit a slow, underhand softball pitch so that he could stand up to the boys who had been taunting him. 4. It was clear that Turner's mother understood her son's plight when she found appropriate clothes for him to wear for the baseball game, instead of the starched white shirt his father required. 5. Turner was amazed because Mrs. Hurd was giving him advice on what to do the next time he got into a fight with Willis instead of telling him not to fight and act like the minister's son. 6. Turner felt comfortable, free, and as if he were at home on the island. In contrast to his arrival in Phippsburg, Turner was welcomed to the island and treated as if he might someday belong there. 7. Mr. Stonecrop persuaded Reverend Buckminster to his point of view using two arguments. First, he pointed out that if something wasn't done to rescue the town from economic collapse, then the young people of the town, like Turner, would have no future. Second, he revealed that Turner had been socializing with "undesirable" elements on the island. Turner felt like a prop because Mr. Stonecrop would not let him explain what really happened. Instead, he insinuated that what Turner had done was wrong and dangerous to him and to his family.

Chapter 5

Vocabulary: 1. b 2. d 3. a 4. c 5. b 6. a 7. c 8.d

Questions: 1. In order to get around his father's latest rule, Turner did not go to Malaga Island, but instead met Lizzie on the Phippsburg shore of the New Meadow River. 2. Turner found it difficult to reach

Malaga because he had never rowed a dory before, and the outgoing tide carried the boat away from the island. Also, he was distracted because he had to keep Lizzie awake as she had just suffered a concussion. 3. While rowing to Malaga Island, Turner encountered a pod of whales that came so close to the boat that Turner almost panicked. But as the whales swam alongside the dory and he was able to establish eye contact with one of the whales, panic ceased and he felt awe and admiration for these giant creatures. His encounter with the whales gave him courage and confidence. 4. The townspeople greeted Turner and Lizzie with silence and hostility. Turner's mother was overjoyed to see him. His father was angry and upset. 5. Reverend Buckminster accused Turner of being impertinent when Turner suggested that it was the elders of Phippsburg who were controlling his father's perceptions of the inhabitants of Malaga. 6. Reverend Buckminster told Mr. Stonecrop that the congregation must think what it will. But after Mr. Stonecrop left, he pondered Mr. Stonecrop's threat.

Chapters 6, 7

Vocabulary: Across–1. haughty 3. hero 4. melancholy 5. malice 6. dwindle 9. amaze 10. dawdled 11. exile 12. dirge; Down–1. humiliation 2. grace 3. hymn 5. melee 6. disdain 7. dull 8. eyed

Questions: 1. Reverend Buckminster chose the destruction of Jericho as the topic of his sermon as justification for the destruction of Malaga Island in order to carry out God's righteous work and perfect purposes. 2. Turner found Sundays dreary because it was the Sabbath and he was supposed to stay home and do nothing other than rest or read the Bible. His encounter with Mrs. Hurd brightened his mood when she jokingly told him that he was as wicked as she. 3. Turner was afraid that Mrs. Cobb might die while he was playing, so he tried to choose hymns that would not remind her of death. 4. Reverend Buckminster slapped his son because he believed that Turner had disobeyed him by returning to Malaga. Turner tried to justify his behavior by explaining that he had gone to the shore and not the island because he wanted to find out if Lizzie had been lying to him to help the islanders stay on Malaga Island. 5. Lizzie risked visiting Turner because Sheriff Elwell had told her that the only reason Turner talked to her and came out to the island was because Willis Hurd had dared him to do these things. She needed to have Turner tell her that this was a lie. 6. Turner began to look forward to his visits to Mrs. Cobb because she was allowing Lizzie to be present to sing along as he played hymns on the organ. 7. Turner's playing suffered when he saw Mrs. Hurd's door and shutters had been painted green because he interpreted this change to a more conventional color as a sign that something bad had happened to her. 8. According to Turner's mother, Mrs. Hurd had been committed to an insane asylum by her son, and co-signed by Reverend Buckminster and Mr. Stonecrop, so that the house could be sold to provide capital for a hotel on Malaga Island. 9. Turner was educated at home by his father who wanted him to have a classical education. He didn't mind translating and interpreting the *Aeneid* by Virgil; he disliked reading and summarizing Robert Barclay's book on religion. 10. Turner discovered that the Tripp family had put their home on a raft and they were floating away from Malaga island.

Chapters 8, 9

Vocabulary: 1. leaves; The other words are alike because they all name types of trees. 2. kindling; The other words are alike because they all mean fire. 3. Charles Darwin; The other words are alike because they all name fictional characters in literature. 4. porch; The other words are alike because they all name window coverings. 5. theater; The other words are alike because they all are associated with a funeral. 6. gust; The other words are alike because they all are associated with barn dances. 7. hovered; The other words are alike because they all describe fast motion.

Questions: 1. Mr. Stonecrop wanted Reverend Buckminster to write a letter to the governor in support of the plan to remove people from Malaga Island after a critical story appeared in the newspaper about the Tripp family leaving the island. Mr. Stonecrop believed his master plan for tourism on Malaga Island required good public relations. 2. Reverend Buckminster hesitated because he realized that *The Origin of Species*, by Charles Darwin, was very controversial and contained ideas that were contrary to what many people in Phippsburg believed about creation. Turner had to promise that he would never tell anyone that he had been allowed to read it. 3. Turner surprised everyone by hitting twelve foul balls so high and far that the balls were lost. He didn't hit a homerun because he wasn't trying to embarrass Willis; instead, he wanted to prove to everyone that he could do something they thought he could not do. 4. As she was dying, Mrs. Cobb regretted that she had always had so much to say, but she never found the right words to say to Lizzie. Turner and Lizzie debated over recording her actual last words because they were commonplace instead of being profound and memorable. 5. Mr. Stonecrop and the townspeople of Phippsburg were stunned to learn that Mrs. Cobb left Turner her house instead of giving it to the town. 6. Turner convinced Mr. Eason to row him to Malaga because he hadn't seen Lizzie for so long. Lizzie was staying with the Easons because her grandfather had died.

Chapter 10

Vocabulary: 1. discretely–cautiously and wisely   2. homicide–the purposeful or accidental killing of a person by another   3. lackadaisical–without interest, energy, or concern   4. groped–reached blindly and clumsily   5. grimace–twisting of the face to indicate pain, disgust, or other feelings   6. ward–turn aside

Questions: 1. Lizzie felt that Turner saw things the way he wanted them to be instead of how they really were. She knew that the townspeople of Phippsburg would never let her and the Easons live in Mrs. Cobb's house even if they received it as a gift from Turner. 2. Mr. Stonecrop vowed that a black person would never live in the town of Phippsburg; Reverend Buckminster took Turner's side and defended his decision to help the powerless and destitute. 3. It became clear that many of First Congregational's parishioners didn't approve of Turner and Reverend Buckminster's plan to have Lizzie and the Easons live in Mrs. Cobb's house when they did not attend church on Sunday. 4. Turner thought that Willis was warning him that something bad would happen to Mrs. Cobb's house that night. 5. Someone came into Mrs. Cobb's house and locked Turner in the attic; he escaped by breaking through the glass cupola in the attic and climbing down the steep, icy roof. 6. Sheriff Elwell fired a shotgun at Turner to scare him away from his plans for Mrs. Cobb's house. When Reverend Buckminster heard the gun go off, he thought Turner was in danger and fought with Sheriff Elwell; in the struggle, he fell over the granite cliffs to the rocks below. 7. Turner couldn't contain his rage and fought Sheriff Elwell when he learned that Lizzie and the Easons had been committed to Pownal.

Chapters 11, 12

Vocabulary: 1. absconding   2. ample   3. talisman   4. feeble   5. thwarted   6. dispatched

Questions: 1. Deacon Hurd convened a deacons' meeting to dismiss Reverend Buckminster. 2. Mr. Newton expressed his regrets that he had not publicly taken a stand opposing the removal of the residents of Malaga and supporting Turner's decision to give Mrs. Cobb's house to Lizzie. 3. The remains were reburied because the houses and cemetery on Malaga Island were razed and only white people could be buried in the church cemetery in Phippsburg. 4. The minister was sorry because Turner spoke from his heart, telling the congregation that his father had died supporting the rights of the people of Malaga, and that the best way to honor his memory would be to rebuild the settlement on Malaga and invite the residents back. 5. It became clear that some of the congregation—including Mr. Newton and Willis Hurd—agreed with Turner when they stood up at their pews after Turner spoke. 6. It was impossible to see Lizzie because she had died ten days after arriving at Pownal. 7. Mr. Stonecrop left quickly because his shipyard failed, and he wanted to leave with the money he had been given to invest. While the entire town was affected, the Hurd family lost everything because they could not meet the payments on the loans they had taken out to invest in Mr. Stonecrop's investment scheme. 8. Turner took the boat out because he wanted to see the whales again. He wept for all he had lost—Lizzie, the island, and his father—when he finally was able to touch a whale and look into its eye